THE NEFARIOUS MALIGNANT POET

By

VERNON JB POHL

INDEPENDENTLY PUBLISHED AND EDITED

VERNON JB POHL
Author
Amazon/Vernon JB Pohl
www.mentaleudaimonia.com

Disclaimer

This is a work of fiction. Unless otherwise indicated, all the names, characters, businesses, places, events, and incidents in this book are either the product of the author's imagination or used in a fictitious manner. Any resemblance to actual persons, living or dead, or actual events is purely coincidental.

Vernon JB Pohl

www.mentaleudaimonia.com

Table of content

Dedication

Dedicated to a former fragmented life, disregarded as pixelated recollections relived through moments of tormenting anguish.

Introduction

There is a pervasive atmosphere of fear and distrust in the world today. People who used to be friendly neighbors are now strangers. Wars and rumors of wars continue to rage, yet we continue on this path of destruction.

If you want an accurate picture of what is going on in the mind of Vernon JB Pohl, look at some of the astonishing poetry/stories told in The nefarious malignant Poet.

Portrayed through agonizing recollections, this short book is written in a form of a mix between modern English and Elizabethan English.

Discover how ten short poems/stories elucidate death, life, and beyond.

He who knows not his deepest murkiest thoughts,
comprehends not liberty.

Vernon JB Pohl

FAITH IN HUMANITY.

I Know not hope for thy species;
For they recognize not restraint
toward innocence.
Massacring be thy leisure;
Inflicting agony thy ambition.
Despair is all I perceive
when discovering this species.

Ye be an outlandish gull to hope in that which there is no surviving ambition to be discerned. Thy wicked species slaughter, deceit, and ravage, yet ye hath arousing expectation!

I see not this hope that thy dazed sights behold.

Ravenous are the days of those who perceive not honor, for they suffer no remorse in their deceptive habits.

Thy brief existence be an erratic lacquer on panes disregarded through periods yet to be disclosed, scripts percolating in crimson bloodstains from these devious manners.

This legacy that ye endlessly pursue would not be glimpsed, for thy desolate existence shall be disregarded by ages yet to appear, never to be quoted again.

I recognize not hope for this species ye pronounce humans, for they be a stain in time better forgotten.

From adolescence, I have learned of this excruciating suffering ye submit unto thy ignorant lineage.

This optimistic sentiment thy beliefs portray be a dull deceptive fable thy psyche calculatedly furnish unto thy already vulnerable and sporadic corpse.

Be not fogged benevolent, for thy wreaking habits be that of thy deteriorated manners recognized by epochs disregarded.

WISDOM AND AGE.

Ye be cultivated from youth;
Honor thy elders;
Hail thy elders uncle or aunt by tradition;
Yet thee educate thy youth respect is earned.
Fools are all I observe
for thy teaching be hypocritical.
I've known intellects and fools of all ages;
For I dare not respect
if admiration hath not been deserved.

I speculate not wisdom be accumulated through age, for I hath known fools of all ages.

Thy life judgments be poorer than that of an infant yet ye demand admiration from thy wards. I recognize not where thou obtain thy reasoning from, for this reasoning be ludicrous.

Thy reasoning for thy respect be not ethical.

Respect is earned, not demanded.

Educate me thy life lessons so that thy honor be examined, analyzed to exhibit that thee be worthy of respect.

I demand not that elders be offended, scorned, nor do I say that ye be not worthy of respect.

I request thee exhibit that thou be worthy of this admiration ye demand from thy youth.

Demand not that which thou hath not been worthy of amassing.

Knowledge and wisdom to me are not similar, ye may be knowledgeable of various aspects, yet thy wisdom be narrow-minded through this doctrine ye obtained.

Inhabiting an existence enveloped in moralities deriving from tyrants.

Wisdom is attained through life understandings, ventures made in transcending life through stepping out of a comfort zone, mistakes made, yet concluding from those mistakes.

Discovering that which was not taught from adolescents, and conflicting that which was introduced in adolescents.

THREE TYPES OF PEOPLE

Some Plummet to extinction;
This Would be thy ambition.
Many Soar and evolve forcefully;
This May be thy yearning.
A Rare few choose to abide;
Admiring the shadows;
Reliving trauma;
Preferring to dwell within havoc.

The discretion ye order would be the path thy existence would ensue. This existence has abundant unbearable possibilities, each ultimate option we deem valid agrees to be the direction our existence would pursue.

The artist to our canvas.

Some plummet to extinction, choosing death rather than to live a life of pain, agony, and trauma. This ambition be more arduous than that of life!

As death consumes with an appetite not comprehended by man. Devoured by the craving to sustain the infinite yearning death bestows birth to.

Wanting the path of death above that of life implies not thee be a coward, for the path of death, seizes agonizing courage that a rare breed of human be familiar of.

The excruciating tormenting demise of ones fragile corpse bestows life beyond that of suffering and misery, for we be not worthy of transcendence beyond suffering.

Many soar and evolve forcefully, as this existence be thy utopia. Thy endurance rise with each impediment life hurls in thy direction, for thy strength originates through perpetual fierce trauma ye contest. This absolute resilience ye clasp be thy ambition.

Life may barrage thee with excruciating sorrow, yet this suffering fuels the bravery ye obtain to endure life. Be not dismayed for the resilience ye retain be that of warrior pugilist of ages past.

Ye be an advisory worthy of this existence.

A rare few choose to abide, admiring the shadows. This rare few discover elegance within the raven shadows, residing between that what is perceived and foreign to man.

Ye be the justification of agonizing torment, imprisoned in a corpse not yearned for.

Ye anticipate Erebus, for he orders upon thy title, yearning a sense once more of that which only they can bestow unto them. Thy battered solidified essence infers merely anguish, for this be the purpose , Erebus hails upon thy title.

Snatched between life and death, dwelling on the narrow line between life and death, never to recognize genuine contentment as intended by affection.

Thy heart knows not affection, solely suffering, yet this be the ambition ye symbolize. For agony will not traverse thy way similarly.

Whichever be thy direction, may ye discover contentment within this path chosen.

AN APATHETIC EXISTENCE.

Ye be the rationale for my apathetic existence.
The absolute rejection of affections rendered;
For the survival of a conventional existence allotted.
Days are obscured by infinite reflections;
Twilights tormented by fantasies of perdition.
Sentiments are for those inclined to be deluded;
For ye be deluded by chemical-induced sensations.

Sensations be the chemicals deluding the psyche and corpse, emotions not subsisting in a domain of sensibility, deceiving one in recognizing adventures of souls intertwining in pre-existing designs set out generations beyond.

Be not swindled by empathy; for empathy be thy descent.

I would willingly live a life of tangibility than be deluded by sentiments that aspire only to influence the psyches of the fragile.

An existence of apathy dividends intellect beyond that of ignorance, this existence I would decide on beyond that of deception.

For deception of the heart and psyche is all that may be perceived within emotions.

The initial casualty in the raging crusades of affection is typically the will to see beyond another's falsehoods.

Dazzled by the affection for another blinds the perception required to distinguish between a victim and narcissist.

Months or years later when the untruths and betrayals emerge, we suffer, crushed, and betrayed, yet all the indications have stood apparent from inception.

Blinded by thy volatile imbecility!

Be not overwhelmed by the chemicals raging within the psyche, for this too, as all things in our existence, can be governed.

I exclaim this unto thee, be not misled, thy passions craving solely agonizing suffering.

A stagnant, unbearable, and withering downfall gazing through the lenses of thy spirit.

As for me, I exclaim this in a vernacular ye be comprehended of, I would rather live a life of certainty than be betrayed by emotions that be the product of chemicals.

Apathetic my days will be, plagued by recollections of a foolish youth yearning for affection.

Innocence frittered by the raging desire for affection not entitled in adolescence, devoured by the seething desire for emotional endorsement among kin.

Lust dazing his judgment, ye dupe!

Thy raging volatile seekings would be discerned across panes engulfed in crimson tears.

Emotions gazing at a distance, snickering at the desolate corps vacated in its wake.

Thy labor is accomplished, disregard this corps to exist his apathetic days in solitary.

RELIVING MARCH

I crave not the recollections
Cascading my psyche.
Recollections of moments
better forgotten;
For these recollections devour
what's left of my soul.
Please dismiss March;
As my heart needs solace.
I yearn not to relive moments;
Those moments that erode;
Erode what's left of my spirit.

---

16 March 1992 he was bred into an unexpected life, this he desired not upon himself yet was compelled upon to be born into the anguish of reality.

Mandated to roam this life desolate and ravaged, not perceiving affection nor endorsement among his species, eluded to wander endlessly as stood cited epochs prior.

He recognizes not pleasure nor admiration, merely misery.

Tormented from adolescence, tolerating intolerable suffering, injecting his heart with hatred and desolation.

11 March 2021 he was inclined to confront his destiny, summoning upon death to receive him among death's kin. Recognizing that this existence bestows no elation.

Surpassing his conclusion of descent and terminating the tormenting existence enforced upon him. With Vast quantities of substances, he gazed death in the apertures.

Death received him as kin should, for death understood the suffering man executes on their own. Alleviating him of the misery of this realm.

He comprehended presently that his existence would be that of warranted harmony, never to return to the anguished.

Yet life would confront him with a startling revelation.

3 days later on 15 March 2021, life yanked him away from the rightful rest death would convey upon him. Engulfing him with life once more, an existence not begged for.

Life sought not to bestow comfort, for life recognizes that his voyage has not been accomplished on this planet.

Comfort would not be bestowed upon him until his undertaking had been finalized.

Ripped from death he now strutted dazed, not endorsing the judgment life had executed upon him, criticizing life, he would rummage day-to-day to excavate death once more.

Realizing that the only way serenity would behold him, is to let the insanity fuel the ink to his manuscript.

This corps would one day be reunited once more with his admired death.

CRAVING TIME

Time is infinite,
yet we never appear
to bear enough,
Craving more,
yet devising the end.
Living in a finite spiral
of destruction while time
seamlessly hauls on.
Time summons upon the
demise of those not watchful.

Will there ever exist a time man recognizes the explicit briefness of an infinite timeline?

An instantaneous flash of junctures forgotten as years departed?

Comprehend this! Time delays for no man, the assumption that 'time broadens' be thy descent, for in a wink thy brief timeline would be effortlessly scraped.

Time commits not to exist by the principles of man, for time has no submissive beginning nor inconsistent end, yet thy mortal existence be ultimately governed by that which ye hath no custody over.

Thy immense scavenging for surplus, squandering thy already temporary existence for that which be the innovation of man 'prosperity'.

This immense aspiring comes to be thy murky penitentiary.

Abandoned for all epochs are those that comprehend not the fundamental essence of an ethical and modest existence, being content within that which one understands time provides to the mere humble.

Constantly yearning more, yet never uncovering. This be the voyage of man.

Accomplish that which thy life discovers alluring, for, in the climax of existing, it is satisfactorily to glance heretofore and appreciate time spend than regret moments relinquished.

Be not dismayed when time continually passes, for the vastly fortunate get to mature old and inhabit an abundantly whole life.

For I confess thee this, time delays for no man.

Be not a scavenger of time, as thy petition would surely end in anguish.

EGREGIOUS DESCRIPTION

Thee hath been deceived
from adolescents;
Overwhelmed by conventional
tales of life not intended.
Appointed obscene pedagogy;
that which not intended.
Arise forthwith;
for ye be deceived
by the deceiver.

Arise hastily, for the deceiver deceives customary. ye be deluded to speculate man abide a life of toil.

From adolescence, Extorted in endeavoring for those not worthy of thy time. From inception ye labor, yet be incapably impoverished. Labor to compensate for that which ye hath no deed to.

Ye be deceived to endlessly wail for aid upon that which thy sights hath never bestowed, yet thee endlessly yearn for hope.

Deluded by the exact species who ultimately formulated these adored entities thy essence eternally yearns for.

Deceived to acknowledge the canine has more ethical right than the swine, for they subsist of the identical nature. Ye be swindled in speculating the feline has more right than the cow.

Thy existence is an infinite noose of fictions taught from youth, frequent ye be educated to live a life of esteem, yet thy mentors be the swindlers.

Compelled to believe the cow's milk is created for human consumption, while the cow's infant is slaughtered for tender flesh!

I recognize not why ye be deluded effortlessly, for thy psyche, be sophisticated.

Thy perception of this universe comes to be the sculpture of an artist intending devastation.

Yet ye blindly commemorate the dupe.

Trade away benevolent! for this be the ambition for thy existence.

Thou delude thy offspring as thee hath been deluded, an endless sequence of anguish never to end. Yet ye assume thyself autonomous. I discern not this autonomy.

The greatest chilling aspect of this delusion, ye frown upon one another, speculate ye be more respectable than the next!

Disgrace is all I perceive for thy species.

COMMEMORATE LIFE

It is confessed that life
is to be commemorated,
yet I wish not life upon anyone.
For this life merely summons sorrow
and anguish,
tormenting souls
to the verge of demise.
Inducing solely perdition.

Why would one commemorate life if life only bestows anguish beyond what is deserved? Slashing and shredding the feeble heart at each endless bend.

Twisting sacred souls to ravenous raven evil spirits, this unbearable existence recognizes not mercy, for all that enter acquires a desolate reception.

Ye continuously exhort deliverance, yet thy blazing shattered manners disclose thee be desolate at heart. Jet sludge raging from thy wicked gazes.

I desire not life upon another, for no soul warrants the deranged demeanors life charms pure souls with!

Life snares thee with deceptive elations, taunts thy fragile heart into reckoning that life delivers more than a desolate pledge of affection.

Heed me forthwith! All this deceptive life contributes is anguish, misery, and torment.

Be not deluded by this miscreant that vows contentment of the mortals.

Inch by inch, shredding my delicate membrane, crimson fluid flowing from this vacant corps.

Deeper and deeper the tempted blade voluntarily travels down my sunken vessels.

For this deceptive existence desire not thy desolate life to climax, thrusting its appalling existence upon those not seeking of its despised sight.

Coercing a weary soul within a decaying corpse, required to wander this sporadic globe until this deceiving existence elects that this life is expiring.

I know not affection!
Only misery.

I wish not to honor life, for its deceptive nature deserves not honor.

Behold the ramblings of a madman, this be the labor of thy adored life! Leaving scars and bleeding hearts in its pernicious path.

Displacing a previously vibrant man with that of a desolate desirous man…

BEAUTY AND DREADFUL HUMANS

Externally ye exclaim elegance;
Yet from within thy essence rot!
Ye claim purity;
Yet exude malice.
Heed my impending peril;
Thy existence be insignificant.

I know of people weeping themselves to sleep due to the animosity of humans, exuding pain as a serpent exudes malice from its fangs.

Humans crushing each other for the benefit of their seeping raven hearts!

Their licentious arrogance devours from within.

This is not the erratic life I desire to resume inhabiting, I yearn not to be a facet of this detrimental nature ye mark life, for this is not life.

Abandon me forthwith so that my weary corps may discover warranted comfort within the carnage dubbed necropolis.

Heed me benevolent! Thy brief existence shalt be shredded from this timeline as the covering from thy carcass when a lion tears at thy corps.

Thee perceive thyself as an elusive deity, yet when the fated time arrives, thy delicate corpse will disintegrate as that of thy neighbor that ye judge so effortlessly.

An evident lacquer on a detrimental period that must be agreeably disregarded.

TOUCH OF DEATH

Call upon death and he would answer swiftly;
For in death thy answer would not be merciful.
Once caressed by death;
Existence would cease to possess meaning;
Affection becomes a foreign recollection;
Euphoria departs;
disregarded as narratives once admired.
The yearning for a touch by death once more
appears to be the ultimate purpose.

Oh, how I yearn for the touch of death to call upon me once more,

for the longing disrupts a life I have not pleaded for.

I have been compelled to inhabit this existence, forced to wander

among those abiding a lie and wandering blindly through an infinite

labyrinth formulated to annihilate.

Be not dazed by your ambition for prestige or fortune human, for

your existence is an endless vacuity taught by the very monster's guise

as angels sent to alleviate.

I wish not to live this fable executed by mere mortals.

My sights have been freed by the touch of death, for pain and misery is

not all endowed by death, tangibility he yearns to bestow to those

inclined to heed and give notice to.

Day in and day out I walk this drenched dirt, misplaced in notions rarely recognized by most, persuades to cease this life not wished for from onset.

Words on paper are all my thinkings become, phrases lost in translation, utterances from emotions shattered by a world encouraging destruction among its innocence.

Insanity fuelling the ink to my manuscript...

Has the phrase 'Second-hand suicide' ever grasped its presence among the abyss of emotions scampering through your being? Not wishing to commit suicide or not able to, yet the whole being cries out for some external force to end the misery, this life enforces on a soul not preferring to be alive!

The actuality of this life may be too chilling for most to interpret, this is the justification most humans occupy a life overwhelmed by dread of the enigma.

Lunacy engulfs those touched by death and its pedagogy.

Mumblings of a shattered man dismissed as words emitted by a madman.

Ye suspect me a gull; a senile being; yet the phrases uttered through lunacy be more sincere than those immersed in honey and favor.

Call upon my title once more ye fiend, for thy record be not exact.

I recognize not why thee attended my bedside, yet in the climax vacated without thy trophy, fled without leaving a purpose to thy detrimental doings.

*If they judge You by your past, they shouldn't be
part of your future.*

Vernon JB Pohl

About the author

Mentally unstable, divorced, vegan, and recovered from alcohol abuse, recovered substance abuse, and recovered from self-mutilation author Lives in a small town near the border of South Africa.

I began writing after a failed suicide attempt and horrendous mental health complications that put me in a coma. In spite of the mental health instability I face every day, I still manage to get out of bed each morning, a trial that only gets a little easier with time, but never disappears fully.

Due to the constant roaring war raging within my mind, I forfeited everything in order to quell the disgruntled voices within my mind. I became enslaved to alcohol and substances.

My sanity left a path of devastation in its wake, pushing family and friends away, and losing everything in the process.

After failing to commit suicide, and waking up in a hospital, I realized I had to make drastic changes to my life, I began rebuilding from scratch. Connecting spiritually with nature and what surrounds us, reconnecting with family, and eliminating alcohol and substances from my life.

Founded a company to spread mental health awareness and to show others that there is hope.

Social media

@vjbpohlauthor

@vernonjbpohl

@mentaleudaimonia

Website

www.mentaleudaimonia.com

Previous publications

1. The unexpected life (Memoir)
2. Thoughts and experiences of life
3. Myne Erebus

Available to download on www.amazon.com

1. Mental Eudaimonia

Available on the Mental Eudaimonia android App

9 798882 020422 7